Can Trees Talk

by Janett V. Blanchard

illustrated by George Koeturius IV

To order additional copies of this book, contact:
Xlibris
844-714-8691
www.Xlibris.com
Orders@Xlibris.com

ISBN: Softcover   978-1-6698-6852-1
        EBook   978-1-6698-6851-4

Print information available on the last page

Rev. date: 04/03/2023

One day two brothers named, Anakin and Tristan decided to take a walk in the woods behind their house to explore nature.

Tristan looked at Anakin and said "did you know trees can talk?"

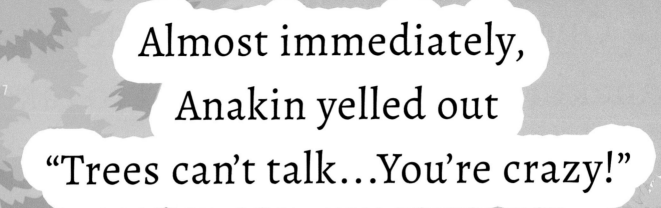

Almost immediately,
Anakin yelled out
"Trees can't talk…You're crazy!"

Immediately, an arguement broke
out between the brothers, debating
whether or not trees could talk.

In the meantime, there was a fisherman sitting on the banks trying to catch his dinner. "Quiet!", he shouted... "I'm trying to get a fish for my dinner, all this noise is going to drive them away!"

"Not so fast!", said the fisherman. "There's a lot of truth to what he's saying." Suddenly, the brothers were very interested in what he had to say.

"One of the fishermen told Jesus that they have been fishing all night, and that they hadn't caught anything. Jesus told them to throw their nets out, and they did it!"

"They caught so many fish it almost sank their boats... Why? Because they **obeyed** Jesus, the fish **obeyed** too!"

The two brothers jumped, threw their hands up in the air, and screamed " I don't want no rocks or trees crying out for me!"

About the Author:
Janett V. Blanchard is a talented author, mother, grandmother, and Christian. She has published several books and loves to use her writing skills to uplift, motivate, and encourage.

About the Illustrator:
George Koeturius IV is a young aspiring graphic artist taking on his first novel.
He is ambitious and loves making ideas into beautiful artwork.

Can Trees Talk

If you enjoy this book, check out more from this author!

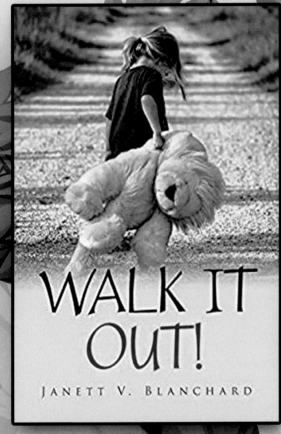

Walk it Out!

The Farmer and the Seeds (Coming Soon)

Printed in the United States
by Baker & Taylor Publisher Services